M Romance

LIFE BEFORE DAMAGED VOL. 3
THE FERRO FAMILY

BY:

H.M. WARD

www.SexyAwesomeBooks.com

COPYRIGHT

H.M. WARD PRESS
First Edition: January 2015
ISBN: 9781630350543

LIFE BEFORE DAMAGED VOL. 3

SEXY BEAST VS. ASS GRABBER

July 5th, 11:28pm

Lovely. I bounce from the arms of one jerk straight into the arms of another. It's a difficult choice between Ass Grabber and Sexy Beast, but choosing Pete does save my ass from bruising and my neck from slug-like kisses. The slime trail on my neck is still wet and has hair sticking to it. Sexy, right? He's got a new nickname now —the Slug Kiss King.

I pick the lesser of two evils and let Pete cut in. He's looking sexy tonight, his dark hair curling slightly at the nape of his neck, a clingy black t-shirt defining ripped chest muscles, and dark jeans that hug his hips in all the right places. The man knows how to make himself look like sin on a stick. He probably is sin on a stick— complete with sexy scent and yummy cream filling. Holy shit! My cheeks burn at the thought. Where did that come from?

I blink rapidly, chasing the thought away. Pete smirks at me, showing off those dimples. I swear he can read my mind. There's something about this guy. Pete makes me want to drop every wall I've built and let him in. I know he's a

Trojan horse though, and letting him in would only end in my heartache. I don't need to add another notch to his belt.

Pete takes my hand and tries to lead me away from the Slug King, who is loudly saying very unpleasant things about us.

"I'm just saying that a woman showing her ass to everyone in the room is begging for it, man, and I'm going to give it to her."

Pete's muscles tense and we stop. He drops my hand and whirls around on his heel. Pete has that don't-fuck-with-me persona about him, back straight, shoulders squared and hands clenched tightly into fists. His voice is a growl. "What did you say?"

Slug King laughs and runs his hand back through his slimy hair. He's arrogant and thinks that Pete is all show. The moron doesn't realize he picked the worst person this side of the Hudson to antagonize. Pete will knock the guy into the Bay and run him over with his yacht.

Slug King grins and tugs up his belt. "I got here first, Pretty Boy. You can wait in line and enjoy my sloppy seconds. By the time I'm finished with her, she won't have a spot on her that wasn't marked by me."

Wow. That was... gross.

Pete laughs as if it's funny. People are starting to watch, sensing the growing tension between the two. "Sorry, but you picked the wrong girl tonight. Back off."

"Or what?"

The Slug King chuckles and turns to the crowd with a can-you-believe-this-guy face, jabbing his thumb toward Pete. Before the guy can turn back, Pete's fist pulls back, ready to fly.

WTF? I just want to dance! Does

everything have to be testosterone with these guys? "Damn it! You two are messing up my night. Cut it out!" I lunge forward before Pete's arm flies and grab his fist. He pulls the punch and lowers his hand. Positioned between them, I put my other hand on the asshole so he can't take a swing either. "Enough!"

I look at crude, groping, Slug King. "Take a hint and take a hike. You don't get to touch me unless I say so. And you!" I look toward Pete. He's stunned, like he's never seen a girl talk back to him before. Hell, if I were sober right now, I'd also be shocked.

Crooking my finger at Pete, I say, "Dance with me."

TWO TO TANGO

July 6th, 12:02am

His blue eyes bore into me. Every muscle in his body is locked, ready to throw punches that weren't needed. Pete stands frozen, his jaw locked and mute. Rolling my eyes, I grab his hand and lead him back into the middle of the dance floor.

Pete follows, albeit reluctantly, still looking over his shoulder at the guy who'd been harassing me. I hold my hands out, ready for Pete to take them and start dancing.

He doesn't. He just stands there smirking. Ugh!

"Well, I thought you said you were cutting in? That usually means you want to dance, so let's dance." I'm shocked by my boldness and try not to show it. I raise my eyebrows and put my hands out again, but he only smiles.

He folds his arms across his chest, indicating he didn't intend to dance at all. "I don't dance. Dancing is for pussies. Speaking of pussies, if you don't mind, I'd like to return to my date. Please try to stay out of trouble will you? Finding dangerous situations is becoming a habit of yours, Miss Granz."

My jaw drops. I gape at him. The words fly out of my mouth when I can finally speak, "A habit? Please!"

"Yes, a habit, as in you are habitually in trouble and attract the attention of undesirable men."

I look him up and down. "The only undesirable man giving me issues is you. I had everything under control back there. You just showed up too soon."

"Really? Huh. Tell me then, at what point were you in control? Was it the first time he groped your ass or the second? Was it when he decided to paint your neck with his drool?" Pete unfolds his arms and takes a step toward me, closing the space between us. My heart beats faster with anticipation, even as my body stills, anxious to find out what he'll do.

To make his point, he draws a long,

slow line along my neck with the tip of a finger, making me shiver. He leans closer to my ear whispering seductively, "Yeah, you seemed very much in control of the situation."

"I can take care of myself." My voice is a whisper in a room booming with music. I don't know how he heard me.

He smiles and replies, "It certainly doesn't seem that way. In fact, it appears that you have no control over certain aspects of yourself." With these last words, his arctic eyes lock with mine.

Part of me comes to life and puffs up at his words. I step toward him, pressing my body against his. "Like I said, I can handle unwanted attention. If you'd given me another second, I could have kneed him in the nuts. Guys are often stupidly close to a woman's knee, kind of like you are right now."

"Is that a threat, Miss Granz?"

Tipping my head, I reply coyly, "That's more action than you'll ever get from me. Keep on dreaming, Ferro."

Pete remains nose-to-nose. "Don't challenge me, Granz."

"It's not a challenge. It's a fact." I snigger. His smile widens, revealing those attention commanding dimples. "If you think your virility is so fragile that a short dance with a tiny little girl may put it in question, go back to your date and leave me alone. I'll find a real man to dance with me."

Arching an eyebrow and plastering a confident smile on my face, I walk past him, dragging my fingers across his chest. I don't get far before he grabs my arm and stops me. I feel victorious, having found a weak spot in his armor. I want to squee and throw glitter in the air.

With a low growl in his voice, he says in my ear, "On second thought, I will have that dance."

I know I should keep on walking. Maybe it's the cozy alcohol buzz overtaking my rationality, or maybe my libido is wildly overcharged, but when I see Pete's challenging expression, I feel alive.

He's conceited, manipulative, a royal pain in my butt and trouble in every sense of the word, but right now I don't care about any of that. I only care about dancing.

"Do you know how to swing dance?"

He moves closer to me, towering over me and placing one hand in mine, the other on my waist. He looks straight into my eyes and says, "No, but I can be an excellent student. Teach me."

The way he says it makes me melt. It

sounds like he's asking for something else, something wicked. My cheeks burn and my gaze lowers, but his cocky question makes me look up again. "Not a good teacher? Inexperienced? Is that the issue Miss Granz?"

Trying to concentrate through the buzz is hard enough as it is, add sexy man candy to the mix and my brain is as functional as a melting glob of ice cream on a hot summer day.

I kick his shin.

"What was that for?"

"Stop distracting me. You make everything sound like sex. Dancing is dancing and, yes, I can teach you if you quit screwing around. Pay attention."

Pete's lips lift slightly at the corners, but he nods, suddenly all business. I have no idea what he thinks of me. I probably seem insane. The music dies down to a faint hum. People are dancing all around us, but they are lost in a blurry haze that keeps me in my own private drunken bubble... with Pete.

Maybe he wasn't totally nuts buying his man-soap from some little Italian town. It's memorable and intoxicating. I should have factored that in before I let him press his body to mine. Add in the night air and the heated room, and it's perfect. I want to sniff him up.

And that's my problem. I resent the powerful way my body responds to him. I'm hyper-conscious of where his hands touch me, enjoying the warm sensation of his skin. We sway slowly as I lead him through the basic steps Ricky taught me earlier this evening.

Eventually, Pete catches on and takes the lead, trying spins and easy dips. He was right. He is an excellent student, learning quickly. His body moves with confidence, and he's not afraid to use his hips, making me putty in his hands. My body is his to do with as he pleases and I follow obediently.

"You lied," I say accusatorially as he brings me in from a spin. Our bodies are pressed together, hot and slick, with nothing but clothing separating us. "You've swing danced before, haven't you?"

Pete shakes his head, wiping a bead of sweat from his brow. "No, but I took ballroom dancing lessons. We all did, and we all hated it, except for my cousin Nick. His enjoyment of it only proves my point that dancing is for pussies."

"Well, add another pussy to the family." I'm mortified after it comes out. "That sounded better in my head."

Pete laughs. "I would think so, unless

you're propositioning me for a night of tawdry sex." He spins me out and pulls me back, twisting me under his arm, pressing my back against his front. "Are you?"

"No," I laugh at him. Before I can look over my shoulder, he spins me out and we're back into position. I can't deny it, there's a magnetic pull toward him and I can't understand why. Pete's not my type. At all.

After a few more moves, I realize we are dancing much too slowly for the song that's playing. I follow his lead, spinning in and out, pressing myself against him when he pulls me closer, wrapping my legs around his hips when he guides me to do so. This is no longer swing dancing; it's more like a slow tango. I try to take over the lead, but he doesn't let me.

Our bodies glisten with sweat, mostly from the hot summer night and dancing, but some of it from being so close to each other. I don't remember being this close to Ricky when he was teaching me.

Pete's hips sway into mine, back and forth, slowly swerving, his hand splayed very low on my back, keeping me close to him. It's exquisite and wrong all at the same time. I try to put distance between us, but he's too strong and he keeps me there, much too close to his body. He knows how to lead and no matter how hard I try, he twists my wrists and puts me back into position—the position he wants me—close.

As he twists my wrist and pushes it into my back, I return to his chest, to that spot that's so close to sex it makes my heart pound as if we were. His front is pressed against mine, his hands holding me in place, exquisitely positioned.

His voice sounds heated, like he feels

the connection between us as well. "You wanted to dance, Gina. No backing out now." A couple strands of silky brown hair flop down on his forehead, almost hiding his eyes. He flicks his head back in the sexiest move I've ever seen. If only he came with a rewind button. I'd replay that move over and over again.

Taking me by surprise, he lowers me down into a slow and languid dip, his eyes roaming my body. I let my head fall back and close my eyes, feeling the heat of his body close to mine. When I open my eyes again, I see him placing one of his hands next to my cheek, hovering above my skin, but not touching.

I try to wriggle out of his grasp, but realize if I succeed, I'll fall flat on the ground. He's got me trapped in his arms once more, and I can't break free. He brings his lips close to mine, but without touching them. His breath feels warm on my face. His hands slide lower, down my throat, passing lightly along the small curve of my breast, light as a feather, before resting at my waist. His eyes follow the same path his hand is taking. That soft touch makes my skin tingle.

We're only dancing, I remind myself. Tangos are sensual, but it's just a dance. Once more, I'm caught with my head and my body in a tug of war, except this time my head is so fuzzy it's at a disadvantage. My body wants to arch into his hand, to feel more of him, but my head is telling me to stop this dance right now. As long as I don't act on my impulses, I'll be fine.

But this is torture. He's touching me, but he isn't. I want him to, but I don't.

Clinging to his shoulders, I squeeze once, feeling the hard muscles as they contract underneath his dark fitted t-shirt.

His other hand holds my lower back firmly, and his thumb starts to rub tiny circles. Sparks shoot through me, down to where they shouldn't be. When his hand reaches my thigh, he brings it up, wrapping my leg around his hip, my other leg fully extended.

When his eyes meet mine again, time seems to freeze around us. Who is he? He dances like he does everything else, passionately. He found my weakness, my dreamy guy button. A man who can dance, who can move and counter move with a woman like he owns her, but knows he can still lose her—that's rare. Pete's moves show he knows that damn well, but this Pete doesn't mesh with what I know of him.

We need to stop. There's no longer an innocent, flirtatious feel to our dance. This is pure seduction, and I have a boyfriend.

A little too breathlessly, I ask, "Don't you have a date?"

He looks down at my lips, and I think he's going to kiss me.

Don't kiss him back, Gina, I think to myself. It's poison. One kiss will never be enough and he knows it.

With a soft voice, he answers, "Maybe. Don't you have a boyfriend?"

Say it, Gina. Say yes.

Bells are going off left and right in my head, but my body freezes. What am I doing? I need to take a step back. This man in front of me is intoxicating and the worst kind of trouble, especially in this state. Alcohol bottles should come with warning labels that say, "Don't drink and dance with Pete Ferro."

"Maybe." I want so badly to admit I'm still spoken for—I can't cheat on Anthony. But a part of me wants to hang on to the flirting and the thrill I feel when I'm with Pete. Why can't I feel this way around Anthony? Why can't Anthony look at me like this, with eyes that threaten to devour me? Pete starts to distance himself, slowly pulling us out of the dip.

Then everything goes to Hell.

ASSFACE

July 6th, 12:36am

Before we are upright, a flash of light goes off, blinding us both. Someone took a picture of us. Pete lifts me up quickly, sets me on my feet, and then does the last thing I expect: he pushes me away like I'm trash. I stagger back and grimace at him.

"What?"

"Get away from me." Pete says with anger in his voice, flicking his hand away like I'm worthless.

What the hell? He's pushing me away like he's disgusted with my behavior.

Since when does he have morals? OMG! I can't believe he's done it to me again. I'm about to say something, tell him off with the rage of a fire-breathing banshee, but I stop. Oh shit. This isn't happening. Some guy has a camera, like a real one with a lens and flash. He snaps a few more shots of Pete just as a man taps Pete on the shoulder. It's The Slug King from earlier, and he doesn't look pleased.

"Ferro, right?" The guy says it in a condescending tone, like "Ferro" is the worst insult imaginable, like the name is vile or infected with corruption. Well, he kind of has a point there; the family has a reputation. But for some reason, the insult feels wrong.

Pete came to my rescue twice in one week. Although, in my defense, I was totally going to give Jerkazoid an acute case of Kickedballsitis. Too much to drink seems to conjure middle school Gina talk.

Pete's back is to me, and I see his muscles visibly tense up. His shoulders square, his muscles cord tightly, and his hands ball into fists. Seriously? Again? I feel the anger rolling off him in waves. Another flash of light goes off, and he looks over his shoulder and glares at me.

"I told you to get away from me." Pete's jaw clenches and his voice is angry, as if I've done something to piss him off.

"Oh, that is so not how things are going to go down!" I cross my arms over my chest and stand my ground.

There is no way in Hell Pete Ferro is

going to give me orders. I have enough people in my life telling me what to do; I do not need another. I didn't do anything wrong. He has no right to be pissed at me. I put a hand on his shoulder, intending to turn him around and give him an earful. He thinks he can intimidate me? I don't care who you are, but you don't mess with a pissy Granz.

As soon as he turns around to face me, Slug King hurls himself forward, punching Pete in the stomach. I jump out of the way, yelping with shock, and putting my hands over my mouth.

Pete doubles over at the waist, and when he looks up and sees I haven't budged, he looks at me with venom in his eyes. I challenge his glare. When he speaks to me again, he is livid and sexy as hell. Jaw still clenched, muscles twitching, his voice comes out more like a yell. "Get.

The Fuck. Out of here. NOW!"

This time he doesn't wait for my reaction. He charges the guy, ramming his shoulder into the guy's stomach. He keeps on pushing until they reach a nearby table and Pete just spreads him across the top. That's when the punches start flying, and people start screaming and taking pictures with their phones.

Sensationalistic feeding frenzy.

And thanks to Pete, there's only one picture of me. I wonder if he barked at me on purpose because he saw this coming or if he's just an asshole. It's hard to tell with him.

BABY DOLL

July 6th, 12:43am

I feel hands grabbing me and pulling me toward the door. I want to kick and scream at whoever is holding me back, but I don't get a chance to. Pete is still pounding away on the Slug King, pulling him up from the table by his collar and going in for another punch to the face.

"Party's over, baby doll. Time to skedaddle." I turn toward the familiar voice and see both Ricky and Erin. I can't believe it! Am I being kicked out of a bar? By the time we make it outside, the fight has attracted everyone's attention. We hear cheering, yelling, and loud crashes as they are tossed about the room, breaking. Ricky turns toward us. He's smiling and bouncing on the balls of his feet like a kid on Christmas morning.

"I have to go back and help break up the fight. You ladies stay here and DON'T DRIVE. I'll call you a cab." Ricky looks toward the bar, "I guess our bar will make the headlines tomorrow, huh? Hey, any publicity is good publicity!" He dips his hat forward in salute, points pretend pistols at us with his fingers and runs inside the building. After leaping over the red velvet ropes at the door, he disappears into the crowd. Seriously, is this guy for real?

From where Erin and I stand, it sounds like all hell is breaking loose in the bar. We hear yelling and loud crashes, inspiring me to picture chairs being thrown to the ground and bottles being smashed behind people's heads, just like in old cowboy movies. The Slug King is probably getting quite the ass-whooping if Pete's fighting skills are true to their reputation.

An inkling of worry washes over me. Though I'm still miffed at Pete for barking orders at me, I don't want anything bad to happen to him. He tried to help me—again—and I keep thinking about the concerned look on his face as he took care of me after the fire.

As I'm considering running back in to

check on Pete, Erin spins me around by the shoulders. I meet her intense glare with mild annoyance. She extends her arm so quickly I'm scared her elbow might pop out of its joint, angrily pointing toward the bar.

"OK," she practically yells, "what the fuck was that back there? Are you screwing around with Ferro behind Anthony's back?"

I shake my head, physically attempting to shake out the fuzziness. "What? No! Why do you think..."

"Gina, I know what I saw. Hell, everybody saw. Porn is practically first base compared to the looks you two were sharing. You just gave eye-fucking a whole new meaning. I swear I wanted to touch myself just watching the two of you."

I wipe my palms over my face and groan, "Erin, ugh." I look around to make sure no one is listening. "Do you mind toning down the crude factor just a tad?"

I start to stomp away in disbelief; I need space. I cross the parking lot and just keep on walking, Erin following hot on my tail.

"Gina, slow down! You don't need to be all pissy just because I discovered your dirty little secret. Wait up! I promise I won't tell the good doctor anything. Besides, you know how I feel about Anthony in the first place. I'm happy you're finally getting some of the good stuff—you deserve to be banging Ferro." Erin is out of breath, attempting to follow my breakneck speed across the street. We step out in front of a car, causing the driver to honk.

After some nasty remark on his part, I give him a one finger salute and he drives on without further incident.

I finally stop at a quaint little ice cream parlor and sit at one of the tables in a huff. It's closed for the night, so the outdoor terrace is empty, which is good. I need to calm myself down and sober up. My world is spinning just a bit faster than usual. Erin sits down next to me.

From here, we have a perfect view of the old building that houses the dance club. There are little clumps of people standing just outside, smoking and unmistakably curious about what's going on inside.

My shaky hands go to my throat, expecting to find my pearl necklace. It's a nervous gesture. I nervously roll the pearls between my fingers when I'm stressed, but my necklace is long gone. My nervous fingers jump to my hair instead, freeing it from its ponytail.

"Gina, can I ask you something?" Erin

is tentative as she speaks. I don't think she's ever been tentative with me before. She's always been the outgoing one, while I am just the tagalong. I turn to her and raise an eyebrow, silently giving her permission to ask her question, but with a hint of a warning glare. I hope I'm conveying the message, "be careful what you ask or I may claw your eyes out." Disregarding my menacing glare, she puts both elbows on the table and rests her chin in her hands, staring straight at me with big, innocent eyes.

"Gina," she pauses, "how long is Ferro's schlong?"

I bend over at the waist, tuck my head between my knees, and let out an exasperated cry. "Damn it, Erin!" Now she's got me thinking about his dangly parts. I straighten and bark, "I don't know, okay? I didn't see Ferro's schlong! Nothing like that happened. Things didn't go that far, satisfied?"

Her posture doesn't change one iota. In fact, she seems even more intrigued than before I answered her.

"Yeeeeeeeeah, no!" She flashes a huge grin my way. Tucking her hands under her chin, she continues, "Nope, I'm not satisfied. What do you mean that far? How far did things go the other night?"

"Unbelievable!" I let out a huff of air. "I was trapped in a closet and passed out from the smoke. Pete somehow got me out, then helped me leave before the cops showed up. We went back to his place so I could get cleaned up. Then his chauffeur drove me to your place. Nothing happened. End of story."

From the other side of the street, we see people coming out of the old house. I sit up straight in the chair. Amidst the crowd of people, I see Pete being shoved outside. The Hulk bouncer-guy stands between him and the door, making sure Pete doesn't go back in. The Hulk points toward the parking lot, telling him to leave.

Throughout the exchange, curious gawkers mill about the entrance, taking pictures with their phones.

Pete brings a hand to his jaw and looks down at it. Is he hurt? Is he bleeding? I'm sitting on the edge of my seat, my hands holding on to the edge, the last thing keeping me from running to see if he's all right.

Pete's eyes scan the crowd around him, finally resting on me and Erin sitting at the table across the street. I fight back the urge to hold his gaze, but I can't look away.

Once he spots us, he heads toward a sleek black motorcycle and climbs on. As soon as he starts the engine, a busty woman—who obviously has a great plastic surgeon and a personal trainer—gets on behind him. She puts on a helmet, wraps her arms around him, and they take off.

I slump back in my chair like a deflated balloon. He's gone off with another bombshell.

"This is sooooooo not the END of the story, Gina; this is the START of the story. That..." she repeatedly points between me and the building across the street, "... was not nothing."

I know she's not going to let up, so I decide to come clean. Besides, she's been my best friend since we were kids. I can trust her.

"Fine, there's more to it." I toss my hands up in the air, defeated. I take in a deep breath. "Things got a little heated while I was at his place, but before I got a chance to say no, he stopped and sent me packing. We didn't even kiss. The same thing happened tonight. I was about to push him away, but he told me to get the hell away from him.

"It shouldn't matter." I look down at my hands, my fingers twisting the fabric of my skirt. "I mean, I love Anthony. I guess it's the rejection that bothers me. It's harsh that's all—and Pete Ferro is a superstar. It's like super-rejection."

I don't care what Anthony's views are on the topic, innocent or not, this flirting business is dangerous when it comes to Pete Ferro. It's supposed to be fun and light. Once it's done, I should be able to brush thoughts of him away like a dead bug from a windowsill, but the thought of him lingers way too long and messes with my head.

Erin remains uncharacteristically quiet,

so I decide to pour the entirety of my torment on the table for her.

"Erin, this is so messed up! I don't even like Pete, but every time he touches me, my brain short-circuits or something. That other guy tonight was handsy and flirty, but it didn't feel the same. It was easy to say no. With Pete? Saying no is impossible. Is this infatuation?"

I sigh, resting my head in my hand, elbow propped on the table. Why am I even obsessing over this? It's ridiculous. He's not important, he's not part of my life, and he never will be. I just have to avoid him.

As if to solidify my resolve on the matter, I tell Erin, "If I keep a safe distance from him, I'll survive. I'll get over it, and life will go back to normal. Besides, he shouldn't be bothering me anymore. It would seem I'm not woman enough for him. See? Problem solved. Everything is under control." I stare off into the distance, searching the darkness for Pete's taillights.

We are both silent for a minute. Then Erin stands up and speaks.

"Bullshit," she says firmly, crossing her arms over her chest.

"Excuse me?" I look up at her incredulously.

"I call bullshit, cow dung, bovine excrement, cow pie, or patties, or whatever the fuck hicks call it. What I saw tonight wasn't nothing. There is no way he turned you down because he wasn't interested. That man," she points in the direction Pete drove off in, "wants you, badly. I say, next time you see him, jump him. Fuck his brains out until he's begging for sweet mercy and crying for his Mommy to come save him from the clutches of Gina, the sex fiend. Bang him until his dick is chaffing. Ride him until his warranty expires, and then tell me all about it in sweaty detail. I want a full report, complete with sounds, smells, and tastes. I swear I won't tell a soul about it." She crosses her heart with a finger, then puts up her fingers in a "V," mimicking a "scout's honor" gesture. Please! She got kicked out of Girl Scouts, and I know why.

I'm past the point of being shocked; shock jumped out the window of a ten-story building and became a puddle of goo on the sidewalk below. I search for a proper retort, but remain silent. There is absofreakinlutely no way I'm following her advice on this.

From across the street, I see Ricky running toward us. He's ditched his hat, and his suspenders are hanging from his pants, no longer over his shoulders, but he still looks... dapper.

"Hey, dolls! I called you a cab, and it should be on its way. Gina, you okay there?" He puts a friendly, reassuring hand on my shoulder and looks at me, concern in his eyes.

"Yes, I'll be fine," I reassure him. "Thank you for a wonderful evening, and thank you so much for the dance lessons. I enjoyed myself for the first time in a long time."

Ricky stands next to Erin, reaching up to wrap an arm around her shoulders. They're the oddest pair; she is on the tall side for a girl, and he's, well, more my height. "I hope you'll come back next week. Wait, let me give you my card." He fishes into his pocket and pulls out a business card. "If ever you want to stop by and practice some more, let me know.

I'm currently looking for a dance partner, and you have talent." He clucks his cheek twice and shoots me with his pretend finger pistols again. Despite my adventurous evening, I let out a small giggle. This guy is too much.

"Sure thing! Thanks again, Ricky."

FRIENDS DON'T LET FRIENDS GET PHOTOGRAPHED DRUNK

July 24th, 8:58am

I anxiously flip to the last page of the newspaper, and then slump in my chair with relief. Nothing.

It's been over two weeks and nothing.

I've searched the internet, social media, newspapers, gossip magazines, local news, and all of them have published pictures or videos of the fight between Pete and Slugger at Ricky's club. None of them mention our shared moment on the dance floor. My face doesn't appear in any of the pictures. If I haven't made the news after this amount of time, I doubt that I ever will.

Hindsight is crystal clear. Of course, it wasn't until the next day that I realized how foolish I'd been to dance with someone like Pete in public, surrounded by so many witnesses. Everyone wants a juicy picture of him to sell to gossip rags. According to Erin, many people observed our moment of mutual attraction. Well, what appeared to be a moment of mutual attraction. The jury is still out on the mutual part. Then to be standing right beside him when he was ready to throw a punch wasn't the smartest thing I've done either. People were taking pictures that night with their cell phones, and I noticed, but it never dawned on me that those pictures could go public.

The thought of seeing our sweaty bodies tangled together in that hot dance burns in my mind. My face would permanently turn red if something like that hit the gossip pages. I push the thoughts aside.

Over the past two weeks, I've written countless imaginary headlines, mentally preparing myself to read insulting stuff like "Ferro Seen With Mousy Girl: Has He Lost His Touch?" Or "Ferro Downgrades to Girl Next Door," or, my all-time favorite, "Wallflower: Is It the New Slutty?" Luckily, I don't have to worry about that. I've done daily searches of all the possible places the information could have leaked, but I come up empty-handed every time.

The knot in my stomach releases and I let out a rush of breath. I should feel at ease, but still. It's a little bit disappointing that no one noticed us, that I wasn't worth mentioning. I thought spotting the heiress to Granz Textiles flirting with Pete Ferro on a dance floor would be juicy news. Sadly, it just proves that no one pays attention to me. They have no clue who I am. What if I did make the headlines more often? Would it really be so bad to have a scandal linked to my name? I disregard the thought as quickly as it arises. I can't do that to my family. And that's the difference between us—Pete doesn't think of anyone but himself.

Folding the paper, I place it on the table in the staff room, resting my hand on the front page. Since the warehouse fire, police have been cracking down on raves. Not a day passes without an article referencing what is now being referred to as the "Granz Raveferno". This mess has grown to epic proportions. Regardless of Erin's opinion, this fiasco is my fault. I should have said no to the whole idea. So many people were injured, Granz Textiles is still suffering from negative media backlash, and my parents are distraught by the lack of arrests. They know their grief was caused by someone, they just don't know she's living under their roof.

I keep thinking that I should turn myself in. My nightmares have gotten worse, and my jumpy feeling only quiets down when Pete is around. Erin thinks the same thing would have happened if the rave had been hosted elsewhere. She says I can't change things that are beyond my control. I just can't swallow that. To some extent, this is my fault, and I should bear the blame even if I nearly burned to ashes with the building.

I grab my "Daddy's Little Princess" mug. It's cotton candy pink with a glittery tiara on it and looks like it should hold large doses of Pepto-Bismol instead of coffee. Dad put it on my desk as a "welcome to the company" gift when I first started my internship in the finance department. It's tacky, but it's not like I can hide it or throw it away. He'd be crushed.

After I fill my mug with fresh coffee and a splash of milk, I head over to my cubicle where new and exciting spreadsheets await. Oh boy. Numbers. Somebody hold me down before I lose all self-control and dance on the desktops. When did I become so sarcastic?

I nod to a couple of colleagues. The flurry of activity has died down in the office, making my day-to-day seem normal. Outside of work, I've been avoiding my parents' house as much as possible, making Erin's offer to move in and be roomies all the more tempting.

Outside of Erin's apartment, the swing club has become my second home. It isn't open for business every evening, but Ricky lets me and Erin go in whenever we want. Ricky and I have been practicing more advanced dance moves. The rush is amazing.

When Ricky is either busy with administrative stuff or locks himself in the office with Erin for sexy times, I use the dance floor to practice ballet. On the nights that the bar is open, I offer to help newbies get started, coaxing them out of their seats and showing them basic steps.

It's weird, because a few weeks ago I would have been the one glued to my seat. Now I'm pulling people up and showing them how to rock-step their way into a dance that leaves you grinning and breathless. The rush is real, and the way my heart races in my chest reminds me of the times I've been around Pete. Every time the thought emerges, I banish it again. There's no point in dwelling on that unless I want my heart broken and scattered across Rockefeller Center.

Ricky still jumps over the bar to dance with me throughout the evening. I tried to do it once and caught my heel on the rail. Faceplant. It was a display of spectacular dorkdom. Seriously. They should give me a cloak and tiara for that move. I'm lucky I didn't twist my ankle.

Pete hasn't come back. I asked Ricky if he had banned him from the bar after the fight and he said, "Hell no! I couldn't pay for that kind of publicity. Ferro can walk in here and get thrown out any night he wants."

As for Pete, my daytime infatuation died down to embers. At night, however, my dreams feature him prominently starring in both nightmares about the warehouse fire and erotic visions of him doing unspeakable things I never thought I'd do.

The last time Anthony and I were intimate, I found myself closing my eyes and fantasizing about being with Pete. It made me feel horrible, but every time I pushed Pete out of my mind my thoughts wandered until they came full circle and back to those hands and that dimple.

I wave to Charlotte and turn the corner into my cubicle. She's on the phone, jotting down a message. Instead of waving, she just makes a silly face, scrunching up her nose and sticking her tongue out at me.

I sit down at my desk and start the tedious task of going over the reports from the New York Stock Exchange. My internship supervisor asked me to watch the stock market value for Granz Textiles and find correlations between its fluctuation in value with world news and current events. It's fascinating how a little climate change can affect the price of silk, thus making our stock value plummet. Of course, over the past month, the company's stock has taken quite a fall due to the fire and various lawsuits.

I take a sip of coffee, breathing in its comforting aroma, and I stare at the numbers. Something doesn't feel right. I take out my highlighter pen from my drawer and start marking up the papers.

What I see just doesn't make sense. I drop my highlighter on my desk and stare at the sheets in front of me.

Just as I think to call my supervisor and show her what I found, my phone vibrates on my desk.

It's a text message from Dad: Be in my office in 30 minutes.

I reply: Will do.

Good. I'll go straight to him with this. It may be best to keep this as hush-hush as possible. If there's anything shady going on within the company, it's better to keep it within the family. I hope I'm wrong, but numbers don't lie, and that's what worries me.

I TOLD YOU SO

July 24th, 10:05am

I finish my coffee, grab my documents and head over to Dad's office. When I get there, he's sitting at his desk, his eyes fixed on the computer screen in front of him and talking on the phone. I knock on the door frame, and he looks up, a smile interrupting the focused look on his face. He gestures to the chairs sitting in front of him, and I take a seat, waiting for him to finish his call.

While I wait, I glance around the office, appreciating the backdrop it sets for the important work done here, with it's breathtaking view, supple leather, and modern conveniences. As a child, I knew this was where Daddy worked, but didn't understand the kind of work he did. At school, I would tell people my Dad just sat at a desk all day, talked on the phone, wrote stuff down, and yelled at people. Being a CEO didn't seem glamorous to me. Not when other kids' dads were rock stars, movie stars, or famous artists.

Now that I'm learning the ropes of the business, I have a newfound respect for what he does. One day, that will be me, and I'll have to explain to my kids what

Mommy does for a living.

"Morning princess! Penny for your thoughts?"

"Oh, hey, Dad. I was thinking about how as a kid, I had no clue what you did all day at work. Look at me now!" I motion to my designer suit and the reports in my hand. I've become the young business woman he wanted me to become. Sometimes I wonder what kind of a career path I would have chosen for myself if I hadn't felt the obligation to take over the family business. Those thoughts never occurred to me until recently. It's weird because I was content, at least I thought I was. Since the fire I've reevaluated my life, wondering if I'm making the right choices. It's hard to know until it's too late.

"... going over some of these numbers, and we may need to resort to external funding to complete the testing phase."

My Dad has already moved on to important business matters, so my attention quickly snaps back to the here and now.

He goes on to explain how we're most likely to go over our initial budget planned for this part of the testing phase of the medical grade fabrics. I hold myself back from saying, "I told you so," but really? I did tell him, and he chose not to listen. Now he has to beg other people for the money instead of following my advice and being able to pay for it ourselves. The male ego is ridiculously delicate. The inventor of a jockstrap for the ego will be a billionaire in a blink.

Daddy continues, "So we're going to have a little function at the house next week. We'll invite potential investors, and I would like you to be at Anthony's side while he charms the money out of investors' wallets."

Great. I've been reduced to arm candy. I'll be the demure gentlewoman standing by her man's side while he woos potential investors. The message is crystal clear. I will not be a part of the Granz Textiles team during this function. They won't give me a chance to talk business. I will be Anthony's date and my father's daughter, not the future CEO.

Rage bubbles up, and I feel my eyes begin to prickle, but I refuse to cry in front of my father. I refuse to show him any sign of weakness. Crying is such a childish response. Why can't I tell him what I'm thinking—that I'm an asset to the company, not some brainless bimbo. Why did I go to college if he doesn't want me to work? My jaw tightens.

"Was there something you wanted to show me, Regina?" Dad motions to the papers I'm twisting and crumpling in my hands. My fingers have gone white from squeezing so hard.

"Yes there is—please look at these." I try to keep my voice as neutral as possible, even though I'm brooding inside.

I smooth my documents, place them where Daddy can also see them and start to explain, "Despite the drop in our stock value, there's been a lot of purchasing going on." As I talk, Dad taps his lower lip with the tip of a finger. "Normally, that would be an encouraging sign except that most of these purchases are being done through the same stockbroker. See?" I point to all of the highlighted areas on the sheets. "The buyers are all different, but the stockbroker is always the same one."

I chance a look at my Dad to get a feel for his reaction. I'm expecting him to disregard anything I say at this point, so his reaction surprises me. It's not the one I expected at all, but it's a reaction nonetheless.

Though I find it strange, he seems pleased.

His mouth pulls into a bright grin. He slaps his palms on the desk, elated. "This is great news! Make sure Charlotte finds out who this stockbroker is and have her send him an invitation for our little get together next week. Good work, Regina." He dismisses me and sends me on my sweet little way by handing my crumpled files back and returning to his computer screen. When I don't budge, he looks at me, questioningly.

I tap the papers. "Dad, aren't you just a little bit suspicious about this guy? I mean, why the sudden interest in our stock?"

Dad waves me off like I'm talking gibberish. "Believe me, sweetie, this is a positive thing. He's bringing more money into the company." He dismisses me again, but I still don't budge.

"This smells bad, Dad. I could investigate into who the shareholders are to see if there's a link..."

Dad cuts me off, taking his no-nonsense pose. It's his elbows on the desk, fingers entwined, glaring through his eyelashes pose. "That'll be all, Regina. Go back to your desk and make sure that Charlotte invites this stockbroker to the party." It's the final dismissal.

He's done listening to my arguments. I take my documents and head out the door to his office. It doesn't matter what I say or do. In the end, I'm just sitting here, biding my time until he decides to retire and hand the reins over to me. Until then, my opinion counts for nothing.

As I walk through the doorway, I stop

and ask, "Dad? How's the investigation going? Have they arrested anyone yet? Do they have any names?"

Dad rocks back on his chair, and the smile swiftly falls from his lips. The warehouse fire is not his favorite topic of discussion, and I shouldn't bring it up, but I have to know.

"Things have been quiet, other than a couple of new lawsuits filed against us. They're still waiting for the final witness to come out of his coma before making arrests. It seems he may be one of the guys responsible for lighting the fire. He has a criminal history of assault and several misdemeanors. We're hoping he does wake up so he can shed some light on what happened." Dad clears his throat and shuffles some papers on his desk. "Try not to worry too much about it, Gina. They'll find the culprits. And when they do, they will pay for what they did."

I look down, unable to face my father anymore. I nod once and leave, closing the door behind me. I feel guilty for all the wounded people, for lying to my parents, for breaking the law, for putting our company through hell. I even feel guilt over the guy in the coma, even if he is the arsonist.

My conscience says I should confess and face the consequences of my actions, but I got a second chance at life. I should be dead. I should have died that night. Too many mixed emotions skew my thoughts, making my mind a tangled mess. Logic left the party a long time ago. It's just me, and remorse and guilt, and the naive hope that somehow this will be all right in the end, that this isn't my fault. The fact is, until coma guy wakes up, I won't know.

SHOWTIME

August 3rd, 4:56pm

Looking into the mirror, I gently insert my second earring; a freshwater cultured pearl on a sterling silver stem, simple yet elegant. I study my reflection, critiquing each aspect of my appearance, silently judging whether I will meet Daddy's standard for class and sophistication.

I'm so tired of playing Regina, the dutiful daughter. My entire life has been an act, a show, a supporting role for the people surrounding me with dominant agendas. Whether I'm on stage or mingling in society, it's all the same.

Act a certain way, Regina.

Say certain things, Regina.

Give them the show that they've come to see, Regina.

Tonight I'll make everyone believe I'm having the time of my life, though I'd rather be swing dancing at Ricky's club. This past month has been a whirlwind of both exciting and traumatic events. Despite my mistakes, I'm finally discovering who I am and who I long to be, and that young woman is within reach. She's strong and smart—ready to live her life.

I assess the stranger in the mirror once more, my eyes lingering on her virginal white silk dress with distaste. She looks prim, modest, and pure. I've lived with her my entire life, but it's only recently that she's become a stranger to me. I don't want to be her anymore.

I want to be bold, to be brave, to be outgoing and reckless. Suddenly I feel as if I'm gasping for breath, gasping for life. I feel like there's an hourglass in front of me and time is running out. Until now, I've lived selflessly, putting everyone else first and myself last. Each grain of sand is falling through the hole screaming for me to be selfish. Take control already and stop dancing for them. Stop the act.

Just stop.

My phone vibrates. It's a text from Mom telling me to hurry down and help greet our guests. I put my mental argument on hold for later. Those are questions I'm going to have to answer. Maybe it was the fire or maybe it's because I've finally grown up, but I can't go on pretending to be someone I'm not.

I strap on an elegant pair of high-heeled sandals, straighten my back, lift my chin and walk down the stairs. I walk through the French doors, steeling myself against my mutinous thoughts as I join my parents in the garden.

BROWN NOSERS' PARADISE

August 3rd, 5:08pm

The late summer evening coupled with the warm breeze coming off the water set just the right conditions for an outdoor event. My parents' estate has been decorated elegantly, of course. Dogwoods line this side of the vast lawn, giving the landscape a textured ethereal feel. Strings of white lights form a canopy above our heads, providing a warm glow for tables adorned with crisp white linens. A cascade of flowers embellishes the center of each table, their shades of red and orange contrasting nicely against the spotless white tablecloth. A champagne fountain sits next to seemingly endless silver trays of hors d'oeuvres, each offering a mouthwatering aroma. Opposite an infinity pool overlooking the Bay, a temporary stage has been set up for this evening's entertainment. In the center of the event space, an elaborate ice sculpture commands a place of honor overlooking the festivities. Not a leaf seems out of place in the freshly sculpted topiary border of the party area.

Everything is perfect, as always.

I start to mingle with the crowd of

investors as they pour onto the lawn in their tuxedos. It's a sea of black and white, with stern old faces and endless fake pleasantries. Years of practice have made me the exemplary hostess. I smile, shake hands, suffer through unimaginable quantities of air kisses from women and hand kissing from men. I call people by name, making them feel special and appreciated, even as I struggle to remember who is married to whom and try to avoid confusing trophy wives with daughters. It's a horrifyingly easy blunder to make in this group.

I compliment each female guest on some aspect of her appearance—a horribly gigantic hat, a gaudy new hairstyle, an obvious Botox injection gone wrong. Each becomes praise for how young the guest looks whether it is true or not. God, I hate being fake.

There are people everywhere. Rich people love parties. They love to host them, and they love to attend them. It is no surprise Daddy's little "shin-dig" has such a large turnout.

The evening promises to be long and tedious, but I can't let my boredom show. I wish Erin were here to keep me from going out of my mind. She always managed to get us into trouble at parties like these. Luckily, Anthony is here, somewhere. Maybe we can make some mischief of our own later on.

I do my rounds, talking about nothing important with our guests, when my mother signals me to join her and Mrs. Gambino, Congressman Gambino's wife. I know what's coming next because we've gone through this conversation so many times in the past. My mother will brag about my achievements. I'll be modest, downplaying her motherly pride. The guest will then suck up to my mother by boasting about how wonderful I am, ending with a flourish of "you must be so proud of her."

It's so predictable.

"Regina, sweetheart, I've been telling Mrs. Gambino about your lead role in last spring's ballet production of Giselle. Our daughter, the prima ballerina!" Mom says with her hands clasped together.

"Oh, Mom! You make it sound bigger than it was." I turn my gaze to Mrs. Gambino. "It was more of a recital than a production. We only did a couple of presentations, and the theater we performed in was modest. It barely held 500 spectators," I reply, shaking my head.

"You are such a sweet girl, Regina." Mrs. Gambino says to me, patting the back of my hand before returning her attention to my mother. "Mrs. Granz, I've seen your daughter dance before and she is talented. I'm certain it was a marvelous performance. You must be so proud of her!"

And there you have it. Brag, downplay, suck up and repeat. Somebody, please, shoot me now!

Excusing myself, I begin to work the crowd again, finally spotting Daddy and Anthony deep in conversation with... Oh, God, no! What the hell are they doing here?

I scan the crowd nervously. A waiter passes by with a platter of champagne flutes. I swipe one and hold up a finger, silently asking him to wait. I shoot back it's contents, return the glass back to the tray and take another glass. The waiter looks at me expectantly. He must think I'm some lush intending on drinking every glass on his tray. Instead of waving him off, I give him a polite smile and walk away, second champagne flute in hand.

"... which is why we are confident our unique product will be distributed worldwide. We've already secured all the necessary patents and..." My Dad is talking up a storm, trying to peak the interest of the couple standing before him. I walk up to the group, clear my throat and take Anthony's hand. My throat feels unbearably dry, and I reflexively sip my champagne. Nerves make every cell in my body twitch. I wonder if anyone can tell. I hope I don't break out into a sweat.

"Ah, Regina! You remember Mr. and Mrs. Ferro?"

PERMAFROST

Daddy introduces me to his audience. The couple turns their attention to me. Mrs. Ferro has an ice queen look about her, from her golden hair to her golden shoes. Diamonds slither around her throat and wrists, with a clunker of a ring that always twists to rest on her pinky because the stone is over fifty karats. Even her dress glimmers, pale gold with a blood red stone—a huge ass garnet—at her waist. Tassels of 24K gold dangle down forming a unique and exquisite belt to hold that whopper gemstone in place. The rest of her gown is silk with a sheer overlay, carefully stitched with golden thread and matching seed pearls. Mrs. Ferro will never wear it again, and there's no doubt in my mind that her gown cost a million or more. They are that rich, and they love to show it.

Mr. Ferro has Pete's looks plus a few pounds, and the years have been kind to him. Excusing a few crows feet and a few sexy streaks of silver in the dark hair near his temples, Mr. Ferro looks young for his age. He absently twirls a fat wedding band that means nothing to him.

Mr. Ferro has a distant, bored gaze about him, like there's somewhere else he'd rather be. I know the feeling well. Mrs. Ferro, on the other hand, studies me with great interest, like she's appraising me. Her eyes scan my dress, my shoes, my hair, and finally my face. Her appraisal seemingly over, she meets my eyes and smirks.

If my nerves were twitchy before, they're quickly approaching epileptic territory now. Even the beads of sweat that were threatening to escape my pores have evaporated in my fear. The woman has always scared the bejesus out of me, but now, the way she's looking me over, reduces me to a rare material possession. I feel like she wants to buy me off my dad and display me as a trophy in the Ferro mansion. My instincts scream for me to run as far away and as fast as possible, but

I manage to keep both elegant sandals planted firmly on the ground, put on my best polite smile and nod.

"Yes, I do. Welcome back to our home, Mr. and Mrs. Ferro. It's so wonderful to have you as our guests this evening. I hope you've found everything to your liking." Game face on and I'm doing great. Mrs. Ferro's smirk disappears, replaced by an odd expression. The only way I can describe it is that she looks pacified. It appears I passed some secret test.

Mr. Ferro's attention has already left the conversation, and when I follow his gaze, it's easy to see why. He's scoping out old Mr. Gibson's trophy wife number five. She's what one could call a gold digger or, if you prefer euphemisms, a professional widow. He's pushing ninety while she's barely twenty-one, but he's a very satisfied ninety-year-old, and I suppose that's worth a fortune.

Mrs. Ferro is either completely oblivious to her husband's wandering eyes or she just doesn't care. I couldn't tolerate a man who was always on the prowl for younger, fresher meat. No wonder their kids are so screwed up, with Daddy Whorebucks as a father and Permafrost as a mother.

"Yes, Miss Granz. Everything is... to our liking." She takes a long sip from her glass, her eyes never breaking contact with mine. Seriously, this woman is creepy beyond words. She lowers her glass and continues talking directly to me, completely disregarding my father and my boyfriend.

"I hear that you are also working on this project?" She lifts a perfectly plucked eyebrow and waits for me to answer. I'm about to tell her proudly that I am, but

Daddy cuts me off.

"Since Regina is doing her internship with Granz Textiles, we've had her sit in on meetings as an observer of course, to teach her the ins and outs of product conception and development. It has been a wonderful learning experience for her."

An observer? I've been actively working my butt off on this project from its beginning! I look down and focus on a little stone on the ground, biting the inside of my cheek until the metallic taste of blood fills my mouth. I can't let them see how angry I am. Now and in front of the Ferros is not the time or place. I try to remember my father probably went through the same thing when he was learning to run our company under my Grandfather, who was even more of a hardass than my father.

I don't realize how hard I'm squeezing

Anthony's hand until he whispers in my ear, "Do you mind not cutting off all the circulation to my fingers? What's wrong, babe?" When I look up, I find Mrs. Ferro's eyes still trained intently on me, even though she and my father are discussing specifics like timeframes and testing procedures. Why won't she just leave me alone? Does she know I've been doing her son in my dreams? Is that it? Has he mentioned me to his family at all? The thought sends butterflies to my stomach, proving how freaking messed up this situation is.

My Dad is telling her way too much confidential information, but I can't tell him to shut up in front of our guests. I look at Anthony. His eyes are searching my face. He's still stupidly trying to figure out why I'm out of sorts. It's a good thing he's good looking enough to make up for his ineptitude when it comes to my feelings.

I lean into him and whisper with clenched teeth, "I'm an observer? What the hell? Speak up, Anthony. Dad listens to you; ask him to let me speak for myself."

He frowns and addresses the group, "I don't know about all of you, but I'm feeling a bit parched. Regina, why don't you fetch a waiter for a fresh round of drinks?"

What the fuck? Parched? Did he just tell me to fetch a waiter? I ask him to include me in a business discussion, and he reduces me to an effing gopher? I can't blow my gasket in front of Mrs. Ferro, especially not when she has her x-ray vision still fixed on me. There's nothing else I can do. If I stay, my temper might overpower my self-control, and I don't want to appear the petulant child about to throw a tantrum. The best thing to do right now is go calm down somewhere else.

"If you'll excuse me, I'll be right back." I let go of Anthony's hand and turn to leave. After stopping a waiter and asking him to refresh their drinks, I head toward the pool house, but not before I grab yet another champagne flute for myself. I need to find a secluded corner and be alone with my thoughts for a couple of minutes.

COCKTAIL WEINER

August 3rd, 5:57pm

I get to the pool house, but don't go inside. Instead, I sit on one of the lounge chairs and put my glass down on the ground. Putting my head in my hands, I repeat words over in my head like a mantra while rubbing my temples. You love your family, and they love you. They value your opinion. It's just not your time to shine yet. Be patient. Stay in the wings for now. You'll take the stage soon enough. Swallow your pride and take one for the team. I sip my champagne and repeat the mantra... several times.

Still upset, but my temper finally under control, I chance a look back at the party. From this distance, I see Anthony talking and moving his hands wildly, trying desperately to charm the pants off Mr. and Mrs. Ferro. Anthony is a hand talker. When I'm not pissed at him, it's kind of cute. But now, after what he did to me, it's annoying as hell. My temper flares and threatens to spiral out of control. Desperate to regain control, I resort to a game Erin and I played as kids, where we would choose a guest in the distance and say what we thought they were saying based on their body language.

For example, Anthony has his arms out, obviously pantomiming the size of something impressive, his hands about a foot apart and nodding. I know this story. I've seen him, uh, heard him tell it a million times. It's one of his med school stories from an impressive surgery he witnessed. Doing my best impersonation of my boyfriend, I say out loud "I swear, my dick is this long."

Mrs. Ferro and my dad nod approvingly, while Mr. Ferro looks bored out of his wits again. He's probably not impressed by foot-long dicks. Anthony shrugs his shoulders and shakes his head as if it's no big deal. He's still talking away so I keep on lip-dubbing,

"But the oddest thing, though, whenever I'm with your daughter, Mr. Granz…" He gestures again, this time showing a small distance of about two inches between his thumb and index finger, closing one eye to emphasize the itty-bitty smallness of his subject. I can't help but laugh this time, "it shrinks down to cocktail wiener size." He puts up both hands in the air as if baffled. Mrs. Ferro and my Dad raise their eyebrows, baffled too.

I double over in laughter and try to catch my breath. Oh, crap, that was funny! When I finally regain some form of composure, I guzzle down the rest of my champagne. I don't realize I have an audience until I hear a man clearing his throat behind me.

"Hmmm, makes you wonder why a beautiful woman such as yourself would bother staying with a man with such shortcomings. I'd offer to show you what a huge cock looks like, but I'm afraid it may ruin your expectations when it comes to other men."

Of course, being the well-bred lady I am, I spew my mouthful of champagne… through my nose. Nice. Oh, and ow! Bubbles up the nose hurt like a bitch!

I hear laughing.

It's a beautiful manly laugh, but it's pissing me off because I know exactly to whom it belongs. Even though my fists ball up in anger, my heart skips a beat at its familiar sound.

I don't look back. I can't. Never mind that I have Veuve Clicquot dripping from my nose, he actually heard me talking about my boyfriend's inadequate penis length and boasted about his own impressive size.

Oh, God. Shoot me.

All my feelings crash into each other at once, and I'm at risk of a massive head-on collision if I look into Pete's impossibly blue eyes.

Why the hell is Pete even here tonight? How have I not seen him while greeting our guests? He was probably too busy systematically pleasuring our female guests in the boat house. I wonder if he walks around with a ticket dispenser like in a butcher's shop, Next up for pleasure: ticket number 457. Estimated wait time 10 minutes.

The thought of him with another woman, especially here, in my home, makes me livid. I know it shouldn't affect me, but he has a way of getting under my skin and grating every nerve I have. Okay, so he and I shared a couple flirty moments together. That doesn't afford me a claim to him, and I don't want one either. Still, it bothers me to imagine him with other women; it brings the memory of him rejecting me front row and center.

From over my shoulder, he hands me a napkin, and I take it, dabbing my nose daintily.

Pretending he's no one of consequence, and that nose spewage is respectable behavior, I put on my polite voice and simply say, "Thank you."

I don't need Pete toying with my emotions today of all days. My are nerves already frayed, and I'm afraid I'll snap at the least provocation. I keep my back to him, hoping that if I don't make eye contact, he'll take the subtle hint that I'm in no mood for chit-chat and go away. But instead of leaving, he keeps on talking.

His voice is luscious, pouring from between his lips like wine, "I can't understand why the most beautiful woman at this party would sit alone in a secluded corner."

I'm still patting my nose with my napkin and trying to make sure my makeup isn't smeared like a freaky crying clown painting.

He goes on, "She could be enraptured by her beloved, spending time with the man she attended with, but she's here. Alone. It makes me wonder if she was waiting here for me to find her." His voice catches on the last word.

What did he just say? Did he insinuate I lured him here on purpose? And... did he call me beautiful? Again? I get lost in the swirling feeling inside me and wish that it was real, but it's not. Nothing about Pete is genuine.

There is no way I'm falling for this again. I stand to face him, back stiff as a board, my shoulders squared and my chin up. Refusing to look at him, I snap, "Go use your lines on someone who hasn't heard them before."

"Wow. I pay you a sincere compliment and get verbally bitch-slapped."

"I don't have time for this." I start to walk away while chanting, don't look at him, don't look at him, in my head.

Pete's playfulness is back in his voice. He's up on the balls of his feet, close behind me. "Ah, we both know why you're over here making fun of your man's lack of endowment and avoiding people. Admit it, Gina."

My feet stop. My lips part, ready to whirl around and throw some witty remark back in his face, but I feel his breath blow softly in my ear as he waits—he's that close. If possible, my body stiffens even more as his fingers brush my hair back gently behind my shoulders. My knees do this awkward melty thing where they bend slightly in directions they shouldn't.

How can a touch so delicate feel so powerful? It's an innocent touch, but it feels sinful.

I inhale shakily, wishing I could hide his effect on me. He knows what he does to me, and the way I stiffen and gasp confirms it. I wish for strength, needing to tell him off, but when I turn, I'm mentally unprepared for the challenge.

Pete stands there, in all his good looking eye-candy glory. Messy hair, stubbled face, a tightly fitted tee, strategically frayed blue jeans, and black biker boots--all offensively casual for an evening garden party. I've seen the look on him many times. I should be used to the gut-wrenching attraction to him by now, but I'm not. As always, my body reacts with increasing intensity, an addict craving her addiction. Heat spreads all over, and I want to get closer to him, my earlier anger negated by longing.

I refuse to let him get to me, even though he's already halfway there. "Admit what, Master Ferro, that you're an asshat?" Master Ferro! Slam! He probably hasn't been called that since he was nine years old. I need better material. Seriously. I make an annoyed sound when he doesn't respond. "Stop looking at me like that."

"Like what? Like you're a beautiful woman? Like you're worth looking at twice?" His breath catches like he's going to say something else, but he stops himself. His beautiful lips press shut and form a thin line, but the spell is still there, holding us in place.

Heart pounding, I can't seem to step away from him. How much I'm drawn to this man scares me. I'm pulled toward him to do things I shouldn't do. I've never felt like this before and resisting it is like trying not to breathe. In little doses it's fun, but in large doses it's lethal.

Why can't I see what he's doing? I can't put the pieces together. It's like he sought me out. His words are intoxicating, and once those eyes catch mine, I lose control.

My voice is a whisper, and it's all I can do to keep it steady. "Don't say things you don't mean, not to me. I'm not like the other women falling at your feet. This isn't a game to me, so please stop." Too much truth leaves me raw and shaking. My fists are at my sides, clutching my dress, wrinkling the fabric.

Pete steps closer and touches a strand of hair. Lifting it gently, his head tips to the side. "Don't ask me to do things that make no sense, that defy logic and reason. I don't know how I came to be here tonight. God knows I didn't plan on it—

look at me—and yet, here I am, and I can't seem to step away."

His words sound like poetry falling from his lips. Each word is like a falling star, beautiful and brilliant. I can't move. I can't breathe.

In a very sexy and sensuous move on his part, Pete slowly moistens his lips with his tongue. He lifts a hand and gently sweeps his fingers over my cheek. He wants to say something more, I know he does. The way his lips part gives him away, but no more falling stars. No more poetry. Nothing. He stands there, caressing my cheek, eyes locked, and that's when I feel it. There's a slight tremor in his touch. It makes my heart jump into my throat. My reaction is sudden and violent. I laugh like something is too funny, even though Pete's expression is still filled with adoration.

"I'm so incredibly stupid." I step back

and break the trance between us. The lusty fog clears and I blather on, ranting. "All this time I've been thinking why does he like me? Why is Pete Ferro bothering to see me when no one else does. I'm unsubstantial. A shadow has more weight than I do, and yet the most powerful bachelor in New York is drooling over me?" My voice is so high when I say the last word that it cracks.

Pete lifts his hands in a plea and steps toward me. "Gina, you don't—"

I point a finger at him as angry tears flow from my eyes, "No, Pete. You don't. Don't talk to me, don't come near me again. I'm not a conquest, and if you care about me in the slightest, you'll stay the hell away. But you don't, do you? You never care about any of them. My heart's not made of ice, sorry. I don't cheat and I sure as hell will never submit to your caustic charm. Say anything you like. Give me every dapper look you have and douse me with your charming smile tuned to full blast. You'll never have me."

COMING SOON:

LIFE BEFORE DAMAGED 4
THE FERRO FAMILY

*****

To ensure you don't miss H.M. Ward's next book, text AWESOMEBOOKS (one word) to 22828 and you will get an email reminder on release day.

*****

Want to talk to other fans?
Go to Facebook and join the discussion!

COVER REVEAL:

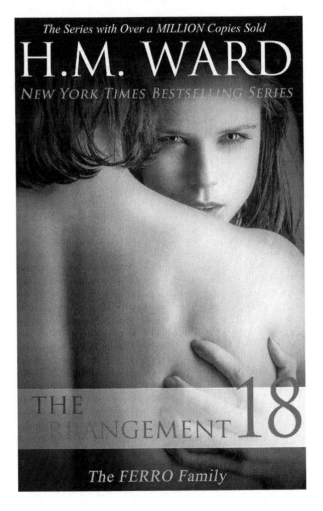

The Series with Over a MILLION Copies Sold

H.M. WARD

NEW YORK TIMES BESTSELLING SERIES

THE
ARRANGEMENT 18

The FERRO Family

MORE FERRO FAMILY BOOKS

NICK FERRO
~THE WEDDING CONTRACT~
*****

BRYAN FERRO
~THE PROPOSITION~
*****

SEAN FERRO
~THE ARRANGEMENT~
******

PETER FERRO GRANZ
~DAMAGED~
******

JONATHAN FERRO
~STRIPPED~
******

MORE ROMANCE BY H.M. WARD

SCANDALOUS

SCANDALOUS 2

SECRETS

THE SECRET LIFE OF TRYSTAN SCOTT

DEMON KISSED

CHRISTMAS KISSES

SECOND CHANCES

And more.

To see a full book list, please visit:
www.sexyawesomebooks.com/#!/BOOKS

CAN'T WAIT FOR H.M. WARD'S NEXT STEAMY BOOK?

★★★★★

Let her know by leaving stars and telling her what you liked about
LIFE BEFORE DAMAGED 3
in a review!

COVER REVEAL:

Made in the USA
Lexington, KY
17 October 2016